To Vivienne,

Hope this book brings magical and whimsical adventures! You're so so precious! Hugs and kisses!

love,

Madison ♡

The Magic of the Twin Fairies

Madison and Tyler Faye

Archway Publishing books may be ordered through booksellers or by contacting:

Archway Publishing
1663 Liberty Drive
Bloomington, IN 47403
www.archwaypublishing.com
844-669-3957

Because of the dynamic nature of the Internet, any web addresses or links contained in this book may have changed since publication and may no longer be valid. The views expressed in this work are solely those of the author and do not necessarily reflect the views of the publisher, and the publisher hereby disclaims any responsibility for them.

Any people depicted in stock imagery provided by Getty Images are models, and such images are being used for illustrative purposes only.
Certain stock imagery © Getty Images.

Interior Image Credit: Nazli Ataeeyeh

ISBN: 978-1-6657-0604-9 (sc)
ISBN: 978-1-6657-0605-6 (hc)
ISBN: 978-1-6657-0603-2 (e)

Print information available on the last page.

Archway Publishing rev. date: 05/11/2021

Dedicated to our little sister Lexi Rose

What is it exactly that twins share? Is it the
bond between them that fills the air?
While in their presence, you will certainly see
their unique resemblance.

As Everly and Faye gazed outside their window into the sky, the stars twinkled bright, bringing magic into the night.

As a shooting star soared overhead,
one of the twins quickly said, "Let's wish
upon the star that's high up in the sky,
for one day it could make us fly."

"Girls, it's time for bed," the twins' mother said. They both hopped into bed, awaiting their wishes that stood ahead.

Slowly drifting into a deep sleep, they later awoke to find fluttering wings. They tumbled happily out of the beds, the furniture towering over their heads.

They looked at each other with wondering eyes; they shouted out loud, "I think we can fly!"

Flapping their wings higher and higher, they soon realized that their powers had transpired.

This was a wonderful power, for it was only at night when fairies could take flight. Suddenly, a thunderstorm hit, scaring the fairies to bits. When they flew under the enormous bed, a flickering light lay ahead. It led them to a small door, something they could not ignore.

"Let's open the door; there must be much to explore!" Faye shouted out loud.

Everly reached to open the dainty wooden door that would show them what they had been waiting for.

Shiny coins caught their eyes, making them more curious than wise. With big blue puzzled eyes, Everly said, "Oh my, what's here? It's surely nothing to fear."

On every coin that was there, six symbolic messages appeared:

hope, love, friendship, strength, caring, and bravery.

Everly quickly grasped the coin of bravery, and she flew high above, like a dove.

She fluttered her wings into little Elio's room; he was startled when she suddenly appeared. She whispered in his ear, "You can stand up to those bullies, my dear." She placed the coin under his pillow, flickered her wings, and quickly disappeared.

As Faye spread her sparkly wings, she entered a room full of magical things. She held the coin of caring for a little girl who needed help with sharing. She gently placed the coin on top of little Lexi's toy, hoping it would someday give another child some joy.

With each special coin no child should ever fear; the magical fairies will always appear.

To be continued